The Son of the Cinnamon Tree

나무 도령

The Donkey's Egg

당나귀 알을 산 농부

HOLLYM
Elizabeth NJ · Seoul

The Son of the Cinnamon Tree

Once upon a time, there was a very big cinnamon tree.
Every time the sweet smelling flowers bloomed on its sturdy branches, a fairy maiden would fly down from heaven to visit it.
The fairy maiden would lean against the tree and sing in a lovely voice. The wind would scatter the tree's flowers and send the young maiden's song far, far away.

나무 도령

아주 먼 옛날, 커다란 계수나무 한 그루가 있었습니다.

힘차게 뻗은 가지에 향기로운 꽃이 필 때면, 하늘에 사는 선녀가 계수나무를 찾아왔습니다.

선녀는 계수나무에 기대어 고운 목소리로 노래를 불렀습니다.

바람은 꽃잎을 흩날리며 선녀의 노래를 멀리멀리 실어갔습니다.

The cinnamon tree loved to listen to the beautiful voice of the maiden. And the maiden loved to smell the fragrant flowers of the tree.

So the cinnamon tree and the fairy maiden got married and gave birth to a charming baby boy.

Listening to his fairy mother's music and enjoying his father's fragrance, the baby grew into a strong, young lad. As soon as the boy was old enough, the fairy left him and the cinnamon tree to go back to her home in the sky.

계수나무는 선녀가 불러 주는 노래를 좋아했습니다.

선녀는 계수나무의 꽃 향기를 좋아했습니다.

계수나무와 선녀는 결혼을 하여 귀여운 사내아이를 낳았습니다.

아기는 선녀가 불러 주는 자장가를 들으며 무럭무럭 자랐습니다.

아기가 자라서 씩씩한 도령이 되자, 선녀는 계수나무와 아들을 남겨 둔 채 하늘나라로 올라갔습니다.

In the summer of that year, there was a great rain storm.

First, the fields became covered with water. Then, the mountains became covered with water. The tall cinnamon tree stood bravely on a steep hill, but soon it, too, was covered with water.

Finally, it could no longer withstand the water's strong waves and so it fell down, with a loud crash, into the rising water.

The tree shouted to the boy, "Quick, my child, hop onto my back." So the boy jumped onto his father's back.

The cinnamon tree and his son floated all around the world, which was everywhere covered with water.

그 해 여름 내내 비가 내렸습니다.
들이 물에 잠겼습니다.
산도 물에 잠겼습니다.
높다란 언덕 위에 늠름하게 서 있던 계수나무도 물에 잠겼습니다.
계수나무는 거센 물결을 견디지 못하고 우지끈 쓰러졌습니다.
"아들아, 어서 내 등에 올라타거라."
나무 도령은 계수나무 아버지의 등에 올라탔습니다.
계수나무와 아들은 물로 가득 찬 넓은 세상을 둥둥 떠다녔습니다.

As the boy and the tree floated on the flood waters, they happened to see some ants floating in the water. "Save us! Please, save us!" shouted the ants as the tree passed by.

The boy felt sorry for the ants. He asked the cinnamon tree, "Father, may the ants also ride on your back?" "Of course," answered the tree. "Help them get on." So the boy picked all of the ants up out of the water and put them on his father's back.

The ants bowed their heads in gratitude and said to the cinnamon tree, "Thank you, great tree. Someday we will repay you for your kindness."

끝없이 떠내려가던 계수나무와 나무 도령은 물에 떠내려가는 개미떼를 만났습니다.

"살려 주세요! 우리들을 살려 주세요!"

나무 도령은 개미들이 가여웠습니다.

"아버지, 저 개미들을 아버지 등에 태워도 될까요?"

"그래, 태워 주어라."

"나무 도령님, 고맙습니다. 이 은혜는 잊지 않겠습니다."

개미들은 머리를 숙여 절을 했습니다.

After a short time, a swarm of mosquitoes came buzzing by. They pleaded with the tree, "Oh, great tree! Please let us rest on your branches. Our wings are very tired. If we fly any longer, we will surely fall into the water and die."

The boy asked the cinnamon tree, "May the mosquitoes also ride on your back?" "Of course," said the tree. So the mosquitoes landed on the cinnamon tree and rested their tired wings.

그리고 또 얼마를 흘러갔습니다.

이번에는 모기들이 날개를 파닥거리며 나무 도령에게 말했습니다.

"우리를 나무 위에 앉게 해주세요. 날개가 아파서 곧 물에 빠져 죽을 것 같아요."

나무 도령은 또 아버지에게 물었습니다.

"아버지, 모기들을 태워 주어도 될까요?"

"오냐, 태워 주어라."

모기들은 계수나무 위로 날아와 앉아 지친 날개를 쉬었습니다.

A few days later, the boy saw another boy his own age splashing about in the water, yelling for help.

The boy asked the cinnamon tree, "Father, may that boy ride on your back?"

But, much to the boy's surprise the cinnamon tree said, "No. He cannot." The boy begged his father, "Please let him ride with us. If we don't help him, he will drown!"

But the cinnamon tree said, "No. He cannot ride with us."

Still, the boy kept pleading with his father. Finally, the cinnamon tree said, "Okey. Do as you wish."

So the boy pulled the drowning boy from the water so he could ride on the back of the tree.

며칠이 지났습니다.

나무 도령은 자기 또래의 사내아이가 물살에 떠내려가며 살려달라고 외치는 것을 보았습니다.

"아버지, 저 아이를 태워 줘요."

"안 된다. 그 아이는 안 된다."

"아버지, 저 아이도 함께 태워 주세요. 불쌍해요."

나무 도령은 아버지를 졸랐습니다.

"안 된다."

그러나 나무 도령은 자꾸자꾸 아버지를 졸랐습니다.

"그럼 네 마음 대로 하려므나."

나무 도령은 사내아이를 건져서 아버지 등에 태웠습니다.

For many days they floated here and there all over the world that was everywhere covered with water.

계수나무는 물로 가득 찬 넓은 세상을 끝없이 둥둥 떠다녔습니다.

And then one day, "There's an island!" they all shouted at once. The boys, and the ants and mosquitoes got off the tree's back to walk around on the island and the tree floated away to look for other lands. The boys found an old woman and her two young daughters living on the island. The five of them were the only people left alive in the world when at last, after many days of rain and clouds, the sky cleared and the water began to dry up.

그리고 또 며칠이 흘러 갔습니다.
"야! 섬이다."
나무 도령은 개미, 모기와 함께 조그만 섬에 닿았습니다.
계수나무 아버지는 아들을 내려 주고 다시 물결을 따라 떠났습니다.

섬에는 어린 여자아이 둘과 할머니가 살고 있었습니다.
세상에는 다섯 사람만 남았습니다.
마침내 하늘이 개이고 물이 줄어들기 시작했습니다.

The two boys lived in the old woman's house and farmed the land.

The old woman liked the son of the fairy and the cinnamon tree. He was very polite and kind and hard-working. The other boy, who was none of those things, was jealous of the cinnamon tree's son. So, to make the cinnamon tree's son look bad, he told the old woman a lie about him. He said, "My friend is very clever. He's so clever, that if you dumped a basket of rice in a pile of sand, he would pick up every grain of rice and put them back in the basket."

The old woman exclaimed in amazement, "Is that so? That's really clever. Let's give him a try."

나무 도령과 물에서 건진 사내아이는 할머니집에서 농사일을 거들며 살았습니다.

할머니는 부지런하고 마음씨 고운 나무 도령을 무척 귀여워했습니다.

잔뜩 샘이 난 사내아이는 나무 도령을 골려 주려고 할머니에게 거짓말을 했습니다.

"할머니, 나무 도령은 좁쌀 한 섬을 모래밭에 섞어 놓아도 한 나절 안에 도로 주워 담을 수 있어요."

"그래? 그것 참 신기하구나. 어디 한번 시험해 보자."

So she called the cinnamon tree's son to her and told him to go pick up the basket of rice that had spilled in the sand.

The boy went to the sand and began picking up the white grains of rice. He worked very hard but he couldn't even find a handful of rice.

Then suddenly, from nowhere there appeared a group of ants. They began to pick up the grains of rice and in no time at all, they had picked up every grain of rice and put it in the basket.

After that, the old woman liked the cinnamon tree's son even more.

할머니는 나무 도령을 불러 모래밭에 쏟아 놓은 좁쌀 한 섬을 자루에 담아 오라고 했습니다.

나무 도령은 모래밭으로 가서 모래에 섞인 좁쌀을 줍기 시작했습니다.

열심히 좁쌀을 주웠지만 한 줌도 되지 않았습니다.

그 때 어디선가 개미들이 몰려왔습니다.

개미들은 좁쌀을 하나도 남김없이 물어다가 자루에 넣었습니다.

할머니는 나무 도령을 더욱 귀여워했습니다.

Before long, it was time for the cinnamon tree's son to marry. The old woman called the two boys to her. "Because of the flood, there are almost no people left on this earth. You must both marry and have many children. The house on the hill has two rooms. One of my grand daughters is in the east room, and one is in the west room. Choose one room and marry the girl inside."

The cinnamon tree's son wanted to marry the girl who was smart and kindhearted. At that moment, the mosquitoes he had saved came buzzing towards him. They whispered in his ear, "Go into the east room. Go into the east room…."

어느덧 나무 도령은 장가갈 나이가 되었습니다.

하루는 할머니가 나무 도령과 사내아이를 불러 말했습니다.

"너희들은 이제 결혼을 해서 이 세상에 많은 사람들이 살게 해야 한다. 동쪽 방과 서쪽 방에 두 처녀가 있으니 아무 방에나 들어가 아내로 삼도록 해라."

나무 도령은 영리하고 마음씨 고운 처녀와 결혼하고 싶었습니다.

그 때 어디선가 '애앵'하고 모기들이 날아와 속삭였습니다.

"동쪽 방으로 들어가요, 동쪽 방으로 ……."

So the boy went into the east room. Inside, the smart, good-hearted young lady sat waiting with her head bowed.   The boy married the girl and they lived very happily together.

The bad boy who had been saved from the sea went into the west room and married the girl who was there. They lived many unhappy years with each other until they learned to treat each other with kindness and respect.

Both couples had many sons and daughters. Because of them, the world was once more filled with people.

나무 도령은 동쪽 방으로 들어갔습니다.

그 방에는 영리하고 마음씨 고운 아가씨가 다소곳이 앉아 있었습니다.

나무 도령과 아가씨는 결혼을 했습니다.

물에서 건진 사내아이도 서쪽 방으로 들어가 결혼을 했습니다. 그러나 그들은 서로를 사랑하고 존경하게 되기까지 많은 세월을 불행하게 보내야 했습니다.

결혼을 한 두 쌍의 젊은이는 많은 아들 딸을 낳았습니다.

세상에는 다시 많은 사람들이 살게 되었습니다.

The Donkey's Egg

A long, long time ago in the countryside, there lived a farmer who was very kindhearted, but not very smart.

The people in his village always made fun of him because he was always doing foolish things.

One summer day, the farmer's wife gave him a bolt of cloth she weaved and told him, "Go to the market and look around real good. Then sell this bolt of cloth and use the money to buy something that we can use."

So the farmer put the bolt of cloth on his back and headed for the market.

당나귀 알을 산 농부

옛날, 어느 시골에 착하지만 좀 어리석은 농부가 있었습니다.

농부는 종종 바보스러운 일을 저질러서 온 마을 사람들의 웃음거리가 되곤 했습니다.

어느 여름날, 농부의 아내는 베 한 필을 짜서 농부에게 주며 말했습니다. "여보, 장에 가서 두루두루 구경도 하고, 이 베를 팔아서 쓸만한 물건을 좀 사오세요."

농부는 베 한 필을 등에 지고 장을 보러 갔습니다.

The market was full of people selling all sorts of things. The farmer walked from one stall to another, looking for something to buy. He examined many of the things closely, even though he knew he could never buy them. Each merchant in turn angrily told him to buy something or go away. But the farmer could not find anything that seemed very useful to him.

It was almost sunset before the farmer managed to sell his bolt of cloth. When he got the money for it, he thought to himself, "It is getting late. I must make up my mind and buy something very quickly." He started wandering around the market again searching for something useful to buy.

장에는 가지가지 물건들과 많은 사람들로 붐볐습니다.

농부는 이 가게 저 가게를 기웃거리며 구경을 했습니다.

"아이구, 신기한 것도 많네!"

농부는 사지도 않을 물건을 만지작거리다가 가게 주인에게 욕을 먹기도 했습니다.

그러나 농부는 쓸모있어 보이는 물건을 발견하지 못했습니다.

해가 질 무렵이 다 되어서야 농부는 가져 온 베 한 필을 팔았습니다.

"이제 뭔가를 사가지고 가야 할 텐데……."

농부는 또다시 시장 안을 기웃거리며 돌아다녔습니다.

He passed by a fruit stand. A huge basket of ripe watermelons was in front of the stand.

"I wonder what these are," he said to himself, as he had never seen a watermelon before. He called to the owner of the fruit stand, "Excuse me, sir. What are these big, green, round things out here?"

The fruit stand owner had to struggle to keep from laughing. He thought to himself, "What a fool this man must be if he doesn't know what a watermelon is! I think I'll play a little joke on him."

So, with a very serious expression on his face, the fruit stand owner said, "They are donkey eggs."

The farmer reached down and touched the watermelons with a look of amazement.

과일 가게 앞을 지나던 농부는 광주리에 가득 쌓아 놓은 수박을 보았습니다.

"어, 이게 뭐지?"

처음으로 수박을 본 농부는 가게 주인을 불렀습니다.

"여보시오. 이게 대체 뭐요?"

수박 장수는 터져 나오려는 웃음을 억지로 참았습니다.

'저런 바보를 봤나! 수박을 처음 보는가 봐. 좀 골려 줘야겠다.'

수박 장수는 시치미를 뚝 떼고 말했습니다.

"이것은 당나귀 알이오."

농부는 신기한 듯이 수박을 만져 보았습니다.

He opened his *eyes* wide and asked, "How does the donkey come out of the egg?"

The fruit stand owner said, "If you put it on the floor near the stove and cover it with a blanket, it will crack open after a month and a baby donkey will come out."

So the farmer spent all his money on a watermelon.

He skipped all the way home as he thought, "A donkey for a bolt of cloth..., today's my lucky day!"

"이 알에서 어떻게 당나귀가 나옵니까?"

농부는 두 눈을 꿈벅거리며 수박 장수에게 물었습니다.

"이 당나귀 알을 따뜻한 아랫목에 놓고 이불을 푹 씌워서 한 달만 두면, 저절로 깨어 당나귀가 나온다오."

수박 장수는 이렇게 거짓말을 꾸며댔습니다.

어리석은 농부는 베 한 필을 판 돈으로 수박 한 개를 샀습니다.

'베 한 필로 당나귀를 사다니……, 오늘은 참 재수가 좋은 날이야.'

농부는 발걸음도 가볍게 집으로 돌아왔습니다.

The farmer's wife greeted him warmly as he entered the house. "What did you buy?" she asked. "What do you have there?"

The farmer said proudly, "It's a donkey egg. If we put it by the stove and cover it with a blanket, a donkey will come out of it in a month."

"That sounds wouderful!"the farmer's wife exclaimed. "We'll have to cover it right away." So she quickly went into the kitchen and lit a fire in the stove.

농부의 아내는 집으로 돌아온 남편을 반갑게 맞았습니다.

"여보, 어떤 물건을 사오셨어요? 이게 대체 뭐죠?"

"당나귀 알이요. 아랫목에 묻어 두고 뜨듯하게 해주면 당나귀가 깨어 나온다오."

농부가 으스대며 말했습니다.

"그래요? 아유 신기해라. 그럼 얼른 갖다 묻어요."

아내는 재빨리 부엌으로 가서 군불을 지폈습니다.

The farmer and his wife counted the days until it was time for the donkey egg to hatch. The long awaited day finally arrived. A month had passed. The farmer and his wife, their hearts beating with excitement, threw off the covers.

"Phew! What an awful smell!" they both exclaimed. They covered their noses and screwed up their faces.

The farmer shouted in anger, "What has happened? We have done exactly as the fruit stand owner told us to do. Why did the donkey egg rot?" The farmer took the rotten watermelon and threw it into the garden.

농부와 아내는 당나귀가 태어날 때만 손꼽아 기다렸습니다.

드디어 기다리고 기다리던 날이 되었습니다.

농부는 두근거리는 가슴을 안고 당나귀 알을 덮어 두었던 이불을 활짝 열었습니다.

"아유 냄새야!"

농부와 아내는 코를 감싸쥐고 상을 찡그렸습니다.

"에이, 분해라! 가게 주인이 시키는 대로 다 했는데 왜 당나귀 알이 골았을까?"

몹시 화가 난 농부는 썩은 수박을 들고 나가 냅다 던져 버렸습니다.

Just at that moment, there happened to be a baby donkey grazing on some grass behind a bush in the garden. The watermelon scared him when it landed nearby so he ran out from behind the bush, braying loudly. When the farmer saw him, he exclaimed, "Oh！ A donkey did hatch from the egg after all," and he chased after the baby donkey.

"You're my donkey. Come back here. Come back," the farmer yelled.

The donkey ran into a neighbor's barn and the farmer rushed in after it.

그 때 마침, 덤불 밑에서 풀을 뜯던 새끼당나귀가 수박에 맞았습니다.

새끼당나귀는 깜짝 놀라서 껑충껑충 뛰어 달아났습니다.

"어? 당나귀가 깼네！"

농부는 눈이 휘둥그래졌습니다.

"내 당나귀！ 내 당나귀！"

농부는 허둥지둥 새끼당나귀를 잡으러 뛰어갔습니다.

새끼당나귀는 어느 집 헛간으로 뛰어 들어갔습니다.

농부도 헐레벌떡 당나귀를 쫓아 들어 갔습니다.

Then the next door neighbor came out and yelled at the farmer, "Why are you going into someone else's barn uninvited?" "I'm trying to catch my baby donkey that just hatched from its egg," shouted the farmer. When the neighbor heard this, he roared with laughter.

The farmer finally managed to put a rope around the donkey's neck and bring him home. The farmer's wife happily petted the baby donkey and said, "I will work hard to make many more bolts of cloth, so we can buy lots of donkey eggs."

"여보시오, 왜 남의 집에 함부로 들어오는 거요?"
집 주인이 나와 소리를 질렀습니다.
"방금 알에서 나온 내 당나귀가 이리로 들어 왔지 뭡니까?"
농부가 이렇게 말하자, 집 주인은 배를 움켜쥐고 웃어댔습니다.

농부는 가까스로 새끼당나귀를 잡아서 집으로 돌아왔습니다.
농부의 아내는 새끼당나귀를 어루만지며 기뻐했습니다.
"여보, 앞으로는 부지런히 베를 짜서, 당나귀 알을 많이 사야겠어요."

Just then, the man who had lost the donkey happened to see it in the farmer's barn, and he became very angry. "Hey you！" he shouted at the farmer. "What are you doing with my donkey？"

When the farmer heard that he became angry,too. He shouted back, "This is definitely my donkey. It hatched from an egg today."

The villagers who had come out to see what the fuss was about laughed and laughed when they heard this. They all said, "That foolish farmer is at it again."

The donkey's real owner just stamped into the barn and led the donkey away.

The foolish farmer could only stand there and watch.

그 때 당나귀를 잃은 사람이 농부의 집에 있는 자기 당나귀를 보고는 화를 내며 들어왔습니다.

"왜 남의 당나귀를 훔쳐왔소？"

그러자 농부도 화가 나서 말했습니다.

"이건 틀림없이 우리 당나귀요. 오늘 알에서 깨어난 내 당나귀란 말이요."

구경을 하던 마을 사람들은 배를 잡고 웃어댔습니다.

"저 농부가 또 어리석은 일을 저질렀네……."

당나귀 주인은 자기 당나귀를 끌고 가 버렸습니다.

어리석은 농부는 끌려가는 당나귀를 우두커니 바라보고 서 있었습니다.